WHERE WILDFLOWERS GROW

written by HÀ DINH

WATERBROOK

illustrated by BAO LUU

Today is moving day.

Ba opens the window, pulls the curtains
back, and stretches his arms to the sky.

Má gently brushes her hair and clips it back.

My siblings rush out of bed one by one, smiling brighter than the sun and wider than the window in our bunkhouse.

I stay underneath the blanket.

"Can we stay a little longer?" I beg.

"Nonsense! We have been praying for this day for so long, and now it's here!" Má exclaims.

We used to live in a big city in Việtnam, with narrow alleys
and rickety bicycles, crowded streets and honking cars,
and a beautiful church with two large towers.

I don't miss our busy life then, but
I do miss hearing the church bells
echo all the way to school.

Má sold small cakes in front of our house, and
Ba sold old electronics at the market.

Their foreheads were always covered with
dark lines, sweat, and dirt.

Now we live in a refugee camp in the
Philippines as we wait to be sponsored.

Ba walks me to school before he goes to English
class, and Má picks me up in the afternoon.

The lines on their foreheads have disappeared,
and their smiles have returned.

"We will get good jobs in America," Ba says.

"There are great schools in America too," Má says.

"It'll be the best home we'll ever have," my siblings say.

But camp is already the best home.

I already have a good school with the best teacher.
Ms. Roland gives me the warmest hugs and the biggest smiles.

She has us repeat words and phrases like *hello*,
goodbye, and *How are you?* She says it will help us in America.

All our neighbors here speak Vietnamese. If we stay
at camp, we don't ever have to speak English.

"Those words sound funny," I whisper to my best friend, Châu.

Châu lives four bunkhouses down from me.
We love singing, playing with
pebbles, and drawing together.

On our walk to school, we skip and pick wildflowers—
always enough for a small bouquet for Ms. Roland. She says,
"Beautiful things can grow anywhere, like wildflowers!"

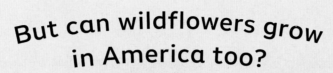

But can wildflowers grow
in America too?

I slowly crawl out of bed and brush my teeth.

Má smooths my pants with her hands, and
then I slip into my clothes.

I run to find Châu.

"Want to play Ô Ăn Quan one last time?" I ask.
It is our favorite game, and we play it every day after school.

I spread the pebbles on the board.

My heart feels as heavy as the weight of the stones in my hand.

We used to smile and giggle.

Now, with teary eyes, we move the pebbles in silence.

"Will we ever play together again?" Châu asks.

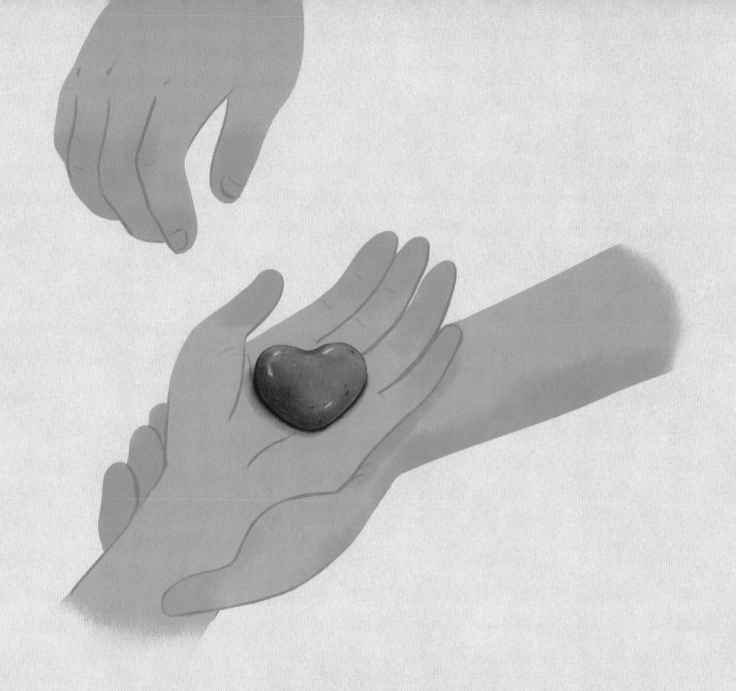

"This is my favorite pebble. Keep it for me!
Then we can play together again in America," I say.

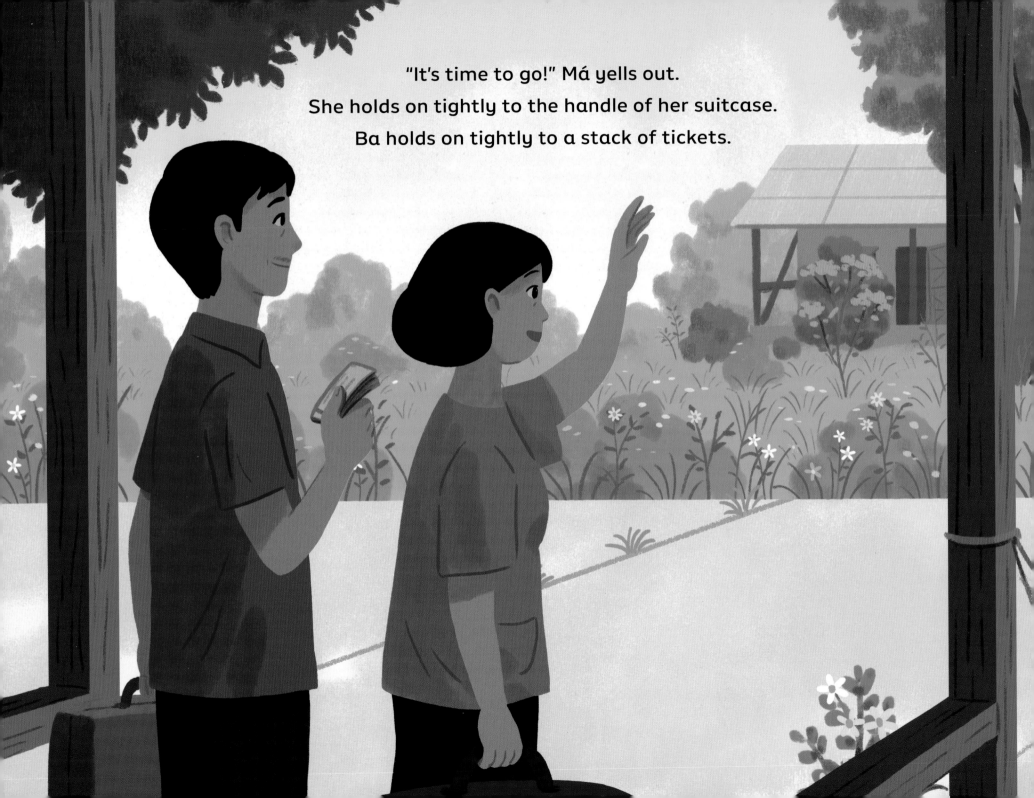

"It's time to go!" Má yells out.

She holds on tightly to the handle of her suitcase.

Ba holds on tightly to a stack of tickets.

And I hold on tightly to the hope that
we could still stay at camp.

"The rain clouds are moving in. We need to go
to the bus station now!" Ba cries out.

I see my sisters and brother with their arms wrapped around their friends.
Their eyes are red like pomegranate seeds.

If life in America is so great, why is everyone crying?

"Time to head to the airport," the driver shouts. "Keep your tickets out!"

I rush to get a seat by the window.

"I won't forget you!" I call out to Châu as she slips a card into my hand.

The bus revs its engine.

Châu holds my pebble in the air,
and it fits as perfectly in her hand as it did in mine.

The bus begins moving.

Tears slide down our cheeks like the rain sliding down the windows.

As camp fades from view, I read Châu's card.

I hold it close to my heart.

I know that even far away, Châu will always be close to me.

I open the card and there's a surprise!

A small bouquet of wildflowers...

just enough to remind me

to keep growing.

AUTHOR'S NOTE

AFTER THE FALL OF SÀIGÒN in 1975, my father, who had served under the South Vietnamese military, returned home with very little savings and economic opportunities. My parents struggled financially and knew that the only way for their children to receive a good education and have a brighter future than their own was to emigrate to the United States.

Through the Amerasian Homecoming Act of 1988, my family and I were granted refugee status, and we were flown from Việtnam to the Philippine Refugee Processing Center (PRPC) in Bataan on October 3, 1988.

The PRPC served as the final stop for many refugees from Southeast Asia before their final resettlement in Australia, Canada, countries in Europe, parts of Asia, or the United States. More than four hundred thousand refugees, including my family, were processed at the PRPC before securing their forever homes.

At the camp, my family lived in a small bunkhouse, participated in English second language and cultural orientation programs, and befriended many other Vietnamese refugee families while we waited. After ten months, our family was sponsored by Catholic Charities and departed the camp on August 3, 1989. We were first flown to Seattle, Washington, and then to Louisville, Kentucky, on August 6.

This story was inspired by the memories and friendships made at the camp and written to thank those who helped my family start a new life. It was there where kindhearted Filipino teachers welcomed us and made us feel that we belonged. It was there where my older siblings were baptized into the Catholic faith through their involvement with the Vietnamese Eucharistic Youth Society (now called the Vietnamese Eucharistic Youth Movement). It was there where joy and excitement could be seen and felt as families waited for more hopeful futures. Last, it was there where so many friendships were made, although farewells were also a part of camp life as each family left to find their new forever home.

Me as a toddler in Việtnam.

My kindergarten picture.

December 1989, my siblings and me in our bunkhouse.

The Vietnamese Eucharistic Youth Society in Bataan.

Day of departure in 1989, our family with one of the teachers at camp. Ba is not in the picture. I am the youngest with an apple in my mouth.

1989, Ba in our first apartment in Louisville, Kentucky.

How to Play Ô Ăn Quan

Ô Ăn Quan (pronounced "Oh Ah-ng Kwan") is a traditional Vietnamese game for two players. It looks simple but requires a lot of strategy. This is a simplified version to serve as an introduction for new and young players. Follow the instructions below to learn how to play!

SUPPLIES

chalk   50 small pebbles   2 medium-sized rocks

OBJECTIVE   To earn the most points by capturing the most stones. Each small pebble is worth one point, and each medium-sized rock is worth ten points.

1 point   10 points

---

①   Create the playing board by using chalk to mark the ground. The little squares are known as rice-field squares, and the bigger sections are called Mandarin squares.

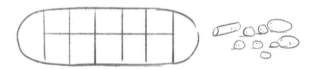

②   Place five small pebbles inside each rice field and one bigger rock inside each of the Mandarin squares.

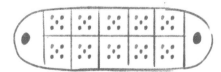

③   Decide who will go first by playing a quick game of Rock, Paper, Scissors.

④   The first player will pick up all the pebbles from any rice field on *their* side of the board. Then, moving either clockwise or counterclockwise, they will then drop one pebble at a time in each rice field and Mandarin square.

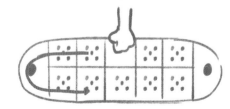

Once the player runs out of pebbles in their hand, they will pick up the pebbles in the next rice field and continue to distribute in the same direction that they started with.

⑤   As soon as the player gets to an empty square, they will slam their hand in it and claim the pebbles in the next square by removing them from the board. This ends their turn.

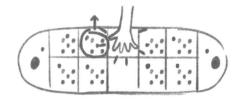

6. The other player begins their turn by picking a rice field on *their* side of the board to collect and begin distributing. They repeat the process of collecting and distributing, as described in steps 4 and 5.

7. If a player ever finishes distributing their pebbles before two empty rice field squares or before an empty Mandarin square, they do not get to claim any pebbles and their turn is over.

8. Keep taking turns distributing and claiming pebbles until all the pebbles are gone or when both medium-sized rocks are gone.

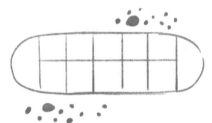

9. Count how many points you each have. The small pebbles are worth one point; the medium-sized rocks are worth ten points. The player with the most points wins.

To Ba and Má,
for raising me up in your love, guiding me each
step of the way, and encouraging me to dream my
biggest dreams. I am forever grateful for you.

To all the child refugees in the world,
may you, too, grow and blossom wherever you go.
—Hà

❋　　❋　　❋

To Mom and Dad,
thank you for your love and sacrifices.
I am truly grateful.
—Bao

Where Wildflowers Grow

Text copyright © 2023 by Hà Dinh
Cover art and interior illustrations copyright © 2023 by Bao Luu

All rights reserved.

Published in the United States by WaterBrook, an imprint of Random House,
a division of Penguin Random House LLC.

WaterBrook® and its deer colophon are registered trademarks of
Penguin Random House LLC.

All of the photos are from the author's collection.

ISBN 978-0-593-57860-5
Ebook ISBN 978-0-593-57861-2

The Library of Congress catalog record is available at
https://lccn.loc.gov/2021056432.

Printed in China

waterbrookmultnomah.com

10 9 8 7 6 5 4 3 2 1

First Edition

Book and cover design by Annalisa Sheldahl

Special Sales Most WaterBrook books are available at special quantity discounts
when purchased in bulk by corporations, organizations, and special-interest
groups. Custom imprinting or excerpting can also be done to fit special needs.
For information, please email specialmarketscms@penguinrandomhouse.com.